Franklin Stein
by Ellen Raskin

AN ALADDIN BOOK
Atheneum

PUBLISHED BY ATHENEUM

COPYRIGHT © 1972 BY ELLEN RASKIN

ALL RIGHTS RESERVED

PUBLISHED SIMULTANEOUSLY IN CANADA BY

MCCLELLAND & STEWART, LTD.

MANUFACTURED IN THE UNITED STATES OF AMERICA BY

CONNECTICUT PRINTERS, INC., HARTFORD

ISBN 0-689-70417-8

FIRST ALADDIN EDITION

Franklin Stein

had been sawing and drilling,
day and night,
hammering, hammering in the locked attic room.

His mother didn't know what he was making,
his father didn't know what he was making,
his snoopy sister Phyllis didn't know what he was making.
No one else cared.

Landlady Twitch, come to raise the rent,
didn't care what Franklin Stein was making—
so long as it wasn't a dog or a cat.
Mean Landlady Twitch,
old as the rickety-rackety house but too rich to have to live in it,
didn't allow pets. Not even turtles.

Franklin Stein's friends didn't care what he was making.
He had no friends.

Franklin Stein did have neighbors,
lots of downstairs neighbors,
but they were too busy to care.

Sarah Hairball was too busy worrying about robbers to care.

Her niece Clarice was too busy being beautiful to care.

The Pfeffers were too busy fighting to care.

LaDonna Metz was singing duets,

and J. Turner Offenbach was too busy
coming and going and working his way up in the world
to care about anybody but himself.

"Franklin Stein!" his mother called
  over the sawing and drilling, hammering, hammering.
"Franklin Stein," his mother bawled,
  "please come out and eat."

"Don't worry, he won't starve," said Phyllis,
  but Mrs. Stein worried nonetheless.
  She worried about Franklin Stein having no friends,
  and she wondered about her missing potato masher.

Mr. Stein wondered what happened to his good striped tie.

"I hope Franklin's not making another footstool,"
 Mr. Stein said.
"The last thing we need is another footstool."

"It's bigger than a footstool," said snoopy sister Phyllis.
"It . . ."

It was much bigger than a footstool.

"Don't bring that junk in here," Mr. Stein shouted,
forgetting about his good striped tie.
Mrs. Stein forgot about her potato masher.
"That's nice, dear, what is it?" she asked.

"Fred," Franklin Stein explained.

"It's Fred and it's red and it's ugly," said Phyllis Stein.

"Ugly, ugly, ugly!" Phyllis repeated smugly.

Her little brother shrugged and returned to the attic room.

"Don't listen to her, Fred," Franklin Stein said,
"They'll like you where we're going."

Slowly, carefully, he lowered Fred out the window,
scaring Sarah Hairball,
who hid her money in shoes two sizes too big.

"Robber, burglar, mugger, thief!" shrieked Sarah Hairball.

Her niece Clarice called the police.

"Monster!" cried one of the five little Pfeffers.

"Eek!" sang LaDonna Metz,
which was three notes higher than she had sung hitherto.

"Shoo!" shouted Landlady Twitch
about to clobber Fred with her cane.

"Fred!" Franklin Stein sobbed as the rope broke,
and Fred went rolling, rolling.

Franklin Stein ran down the stairs,
ran down the street,
ran after Fred who went rolling, rolling
right into J. Turner Offenbach.

"How do you do," said J. Turner Offenbach,
too busy either coming or going to notice anything unusual.

Franklin Stein caught up with Fred,
J. Turner Offenbach kept coming or going,
Landlady Twitch kept running, running.

TERRIBLE

JACK'S TOWING

"Wicked!" shrieked Landlady Twitch.
Two tow-truck drivers and the other grown-ups agreed.
They had never seen anything quite like Fred,
so he must be wicked, indeed, or worse.

Franklin Stein kept smiling for Fred's sake and hurried on.

"Dumb!" said some boys on the ball team,
   but Franklin Stein had no time to chat, no time to waste.

"Hurry, Fred," he said, "or we'll be late."

"Atrocious, ferocious, ghastly giant monster,"
  Officer Foster wrote in his book.
"Hideous, incredibly sinister ghoul."

"Evil," offered LaDonna Metz.

"Awful," suggested a Pfeffer.

"Robber, burglar, mugger, thief," said Sarah Hairball.
"And look! There he is!"

"Hurry, Fred, hurry," said Franklin Stein.

Franklin Stein was barely in time for the pet show.

"Dreadful," someone said as he scurried into line.
"Revolting," said another.

The judge just frowned
and studied Fred from front to back, from side to side.
She studied him up and down.

"Gruesome," said the girl with the goose.

"Original, creative, artistic, superb!"
the judge said to the owner of the most unusual pet.

And just as Officer Foster, Sarah Hairball, her niece Clarice,
all the Pfeffers, LaDonna Metz and the Steins arrived,
the judge awarded the big blue ribbon,
the prize,
to Fred and Franklin Stein.

"Original, creative, artistic, superb!" said Sarah Hairball.
"Original, creative, artistic, superb!" everyone agreed.

Franklin Stein felt proud.
So did Mr. and Mrs. Stein, who now didn't mind
about the potato masher and good striped tie.

Everyone wanted Fred displayed in front of the house.
Well, almost everyone.
Phyllis Stein didn't. She hated lumpy mashed potatoes.
Landlady Twitch didn't.
She said Fred made her house look like a garbage dump.

"Wonderful," sighed Sarah Hairball, who could take off her shoes,
with Fred there to scare away robbers.

"Beautiful," said her niece Clarice,
comparing herself to Fred in the mirror.

"Fred, Fred," said the little Pfeffers; and Mr. and Mrs. Pfeffer
played afraid, which was much more fun than fighting.

LaDonna Metz sang even higher than before,
and Officer Foster told old Landlady Twitch
that Fred could stay right there.
Also no one had to pay rent any more until she repaired
that rickety-rackety house.

Everybody cared now, one way or another
(except J. Turner Offenbach coming or going),
but there was one who liked Fred
just because he was Fred,
and cared about Franklin Stein more than the others.

"Great!" said Elizabeth, who made things, too.

"Nice," said Franklin Stein, admiring her car.

"Is Fred really your pet?" Elizabeth asked.

Franklin Stein held his breath and squeezed past
the steering wheel. "Fred is something to love," he said.

"Are you going to make another Fred?" Elizabeth asked
as she pushed and shoved and pushed her car.

Franklin Stein shook his head, then looked up at lonely Fred.
"I'm going to make a friend for Fred.
"Everyone needs a friend."

Elizabeth pushed and shoved and pushed some more.
The car began to roll.
Fred smiled, and the car went rolling, rolling,
right into J. Turner Offenbach.

"Good night," said J. Turner Offenbach.

FRIEND